The Fence

Vicki Coghill

illustrated by
Stephen Michael King

ISBN 0-439-20839-4

Copyright © 1999 by Scholastic Australia Pty Limited.
All rights reserved. Published by Scholastic Inc., 555 Broadway, New York, NY 10012,
by arrangement with Scholastic Australia Pty Limited.
SCHOLASTIC and associated logos are trademarks and/or registered trademarks of Scholastic Inc.

12 11 10 9 8 7 6 5 4 3 2 1   0 1 2 3 4 5/0
Printed in the U.S.A.   08
First Scholastic printing, September 2000
Designed by Stephen King
Edited by Julian Gray

SCHOLASTIC INC.
New York Toronto London Auckland Sydney
Mexico City New Delhi Hong Kong

Dad was fixing the fence.

The dog got out.

The sheep got out.

The cow got out.

The pig got out.

The horse got out.

The animals all
got out, but Dad
stayed in!